BENNY BRONTOSAURUS GOES TO A PARTY!

STORY: REY ORTEGA
AUTHOR: LAUREN EVERETT FARNSWORTH
ILLUSTRATOR: SARAH RUDY

SK
PUBLISHING & GRAPHICS

SK Publishing & Graphics
2464 Marconi Ave.
Sacramento, CA 95821
(916) 488-4150
www.sunkingpublishing.com

ISBN: 978-097283405-6

This summer I moved into a great new house in Dinoville with my family. That's me standing next to my dad, mom and my sister Daisy. We are a Brontosaurus family, which means we're the biggest dinosaurs in the neighborhood!

This is my best friend, Tom. He's a dinosaur, too. He has a Pterosaurs family.

Tom is really cool.
He has wings so he can fly!

When I first moved to Dinoville, Tom showed me around and introduced me to the neighbors.

These are the other dinosaur kids from my neighborhood. We're all friends and we get along really well.

My other best friend lives next door. His name is Ty and he's a Tyrannosaurus Rex.

At first I thought Ty was a bully because he looks tough, but I wasn't afraid of him because I'm just as big as he is.

A few weeks after we moved into our new house, Ty's mom came to visit and invited me to Ty's birthday party.

I didn't want to go to the party because I didn't know Ty yet, but my mom said I should go to be nice. She took me to the store and we bought Ty a present.

My mom helped me wrap Ty's present and it looked great, but I still felt nervous about the party.

When I went to Ty's party, I felt uncomfortable because all of Ty's friends were Tyrannosaurus Rexes.

We wore party hats, blew up colored balloons and played "Pin the Tail on the Stegosaurus."

When it was time for cake and ice cream, everyone was excited except me. I didn't think Tyrannosaurus Rex food would be good for a Brontosaurus. I worried that I would have to tell Mrs. Rex that I couldn't eat her food.

"Benny, would you like some cake and ice cream?" asked Ty's mom.

"I'm sorry Mrs. Rex, but I'm an herbivore, so I don't eat Pterosaurs milk or Velociraptor eggs," I said. "Sometimes they give me a belly ache. Thanks anyway, though."

"Hey Benny, why aren't you eating with us?" asked Ty.

"My mom says Pterosaurs milk is for baby Pterosaurses and Velociraptor eggs make baby Velociraptors, so we shouldn't eat them," I said nervously.

"Wow, I didn't think about that!" said Ty, surprised.

After cake, ice cream and more games, Ty said he wanted to eat at his favorite restaurant, Dino King.

All the kids piled into the car with Mrs. Rex. I was nervous again because I didn't know if there would be herbivore food for me to eat, but I tried not to think about it.

When we got to Dino King, everyone was excited. I could tell that there was a lot of food for Ty and the other Tyrannosaurus Rex kids.

I stood in line next to Ty and looked at the menu. When I saw the Herbivore meal, I was surprised and happy to find something good for a Brontosaurus to eat!

"I'll take a Giant Nut Burger with baked fries, hold the mayonnaise please!" I said.

I paid for the burger with the money my mom gave me and waited for Ty.

"I'll get the same thing," he said. I was so surprised that Ty wanted to eat a nut burger.

"Hey Ty, that's really cool you're getting the Giant Nut Burger!" I said.

"I don't know if it will taste good," said Ty smiling, "but what your mom said makes a lot of sense. Plus, you're just as big and strong and smart as I am, so I thought I'd try what you eat."

When we finished eating, Mrs. Rex took pictures of all the dinosaur kids.

Ty and I took a picture together in the booth.

Here's the picture we took at Dino King.

Ty loved the Giant Nut Burger and said he'd always try herbivore food when we ate together.

That's how I found out that Ty is a really cool dinosaur and a good friend. He's not afraid to try something new and he made me feel cool for being different.